I0637777

Sucker for Love

Keshia Mason

Sucker for Love

Keshia Mason

I'JALE™
PUBLISHING CO.

First Printing: 2019

ISBN 978-0-578-22143-4

I'Jale Publishing Co LLC
2431 Manhattan Blvd.
Suite C
Harvey, La. 70058
www.ijalepublishing.com

INTRODUCTION

"I can't believe I actually let you come over, well we need to talk Angela, Anthony said.Okay talk then. Angela you got to hear me out. I never meant to hurt you. I never thought in a million years we would be at this point in our life's, and I can't believe you cheated on me with a man a damn man Anthony, you know how many diseases they got going around here. How long has this been going on Anthony and don't lie to me. Come on Angela don't come on Angeles shit you're going to tell me everything. I want to know, or you could get up and leave now. Baby I don't think you can handle the truth, try me, okay. Anthony said he took a deep breath I always been gay. I just was afraid to come out when I met you years back I just knew you would the one to change me ,"

Sucker for Love

Chapter 1: Katie

Welcome to my world Karmen yelled, go sit down somewhere... I'm tired of you taking my kindness for weakness.

I'm so sick of him I mumble to myself. You see, Karmen is the father of my now 6-year-old son. He's so damn cocky and arrogant it makes me sick; he knows how much I love him and yeah, I know he has a family of his own now. Plus, a baby on the way with that home-wrecking tramp. But that still doesn't seem to stop him from popping up every now and then to show how much of a controlling ass he is.

"Katie Karmen yelled!" you got to hear me out, don't you think it'd be better and make more sense if Jr. come to live with my family and me? I mean you're a single mom with, ...before he could finish I jumped in; not by choice Carmen, I said as tears rolled down my face, I will not give my child up to please and satisfy you and your damn needs.

And that bitch you left me for. If you all want to be a happy family, we'll be one every other weekend now get the hell out I yelled. He grabbed me by the waist and kiss my neck, you know that turns me on, he whispered. Stop it Karmen you always try to do this to me, and you know I'm, yeah yeah yeah, he said as to cut me off saving yourself for Mr. Right… well good luck finding that fool the door slammed as he walked out.

I Peeked through my window to see him drive off, whipping the tears from my face. Why do I always fall for his crap, my life took a turn a year ago. I never knew I would end up as a single parent fighting for my child. That cheating bastard needs to stay far away from me.

I need a drink I said to myself my phone started to ring, and it was Angela. Hello, hey Katie girl what are you up to, nothing just finished seeing Karmen ass to the door. Oh, girl, I hope you stop allowing that douchebag to come to get your draws wet plus you know you aren't giving shit up and I don't blame you. I laughed at her, no girl he tried to talk me into giving him Jr again, that fool trying to get off of being on child support I see, Angela said laughing he needs a life, yes girl you know that's the only reason why he wants my child. He wasn't even calling for my child until they served his ass, I'm so sick of him and his bullshit Angela.

Well, Katie, you must stand up for yourself stop playing these little games with him and feeding into his bullshit. If it is not dealing with Jr, then keep the conversation short, stop allowing him to come to your house because you damn sure can't go to his house. He is nothing but the devil Katie baby. You're right Ang I've been weak for him since the split, and it seems like I never recovered. It is so hard to lose the one you love.

I know that girl, but that's why you need to let me hook you up with my boy Ryan. He's a lovely and respectable man. Why don't you give it a try …Angela said to me you know what I think I might take you up on your offer. Set it up honey I said with a smirk and get back with me.

Okay, Katie, I'll call you right back. I don't know this Ryan guy, but I hope he has some good conversation. I said to myself. I guess I'll start cooking.

Jr., I yelled; get off that game and get ready for a bath! Ok, mom? Hey, where did daddy go? Jr said as he walked into the kitchen where I was… he went home son. Aww man! What's wrong, sweetie? My son's face dropped.

I just be wishing and hoping y'all would get back together. Come here, baby... I grabbed him and kissed him on his forehead. I'm sorry you have to go through this and to see you hurt, but mommy and daddy would never get back together, I want you to understand that.

Also, when you by your daddy, you have your other siblings plus your stepmom. "That's not my mom," Junior yelled, "stop it, Junior," I said. You still have to give her respect you don't have to call her Mom, but she's not going anywhere anytime soon. But Mom, but Mom nothing... now get ready for your bath and make sure you brush your teeth. I love you son, and you know that I love you to Mom, he said with a sad face as he walked off. This gets harder every day I hate putting my child through this, but what am I to do I said to myself I am a true definition of a sucker for love.

Chapter 2: Angela

This will be my first and very last time ever trying to be a Matchmaker. You couldn't even call your friend and tell me that you went on a date with Ryan. I yelled at Katie then on top of that. "hold up chick "Katie said interrupting me, why didn't your ass tell me that you used to talk to Ryan. You didn't ask I said laughing Trying to throw her off.

Katie looked at me with a blank look on her face! Are you dumb or are you just stupid?! Neither one I said pissed! I don't want your leftovers. Katie yelled; I can't believe he even mention that to you; I mean that was nothing serious between us. You know me Anthony was going through it I was lonely and drunk, and he happened to be there.

I was very vulnerable, Katie, and he means nothing to me; that's why I thought it was okay hook you guys up. Well, nice try Angela, but that would never happen. I don't want your leftover's; once again. Well, you know leftover tastes good. I'm joking. I'm kidding... I said before Katie could cuss me out. She walked off where are you going, Katie, I'm sorry I said as I walked behind her. I don't even know why he even told you anything about that if he's going on a date with you.

He's such a lame-ass dude I'm starting to see. I wonder why Ashley give his ass the blues. "Who the hell is an Ashley?!" Katie yelled as she turned around, and we met face-to-face. I took two steps back. I wanted to be prepared in case she tries to swing. That's his on and off again girlfriend. I'll be goddamn, Katie said. I don't even know the girl.

"Look" Katie y' all both were going through some things, and I thought that y' all could get to know each other and get y' all minds of these people that keep on breaking y'all hearts. Katie, you know I'm your friend, and I didn't mean anything by this. I was trying to be there for you.

"I know Angela," Katie said you mean well, but I had to cut him off. I'm just not going to settle she said as a tear rolled down her face. Aww, baby I'm so sorry don't cry I'm okay. Angela, at least you were straight up with me and not lie about it. But enough about me, Katie, how's things with Anthony? I don't want to talk about him Katie, too much of pain I start to feel when I hear that name.

You see Anthony, and I have been on an up and down roller coaster. He is my husband, but he broke our bond when I caught him cheating with another man! And yes, I said a man, not a woman! He's been trying to convince me that he's not gay but what the hell do you call another man giving you oral sex. Sure, the hell not straight... we have three kids together, and he broke me to the core.

I went days without eating. I even was admitted into the hospital for a week. Thank God for a friend like Katie. She stood by my side through it all but why the hell she got to bring him up. But Angela I want you to be able to talk about this... I mean that man hurt you so bad I lost you for weeks, Katie said to me.

It was like you were another person. Your kids are wondering where daddy and mama are, and it hurts me to know that I know the truth, mommy going through a lot and daddy scared to show his face because of his actions. I know Katie for right now you have your friend back please don't make me go back into rehab.

You see, I started drinking heavily after I caught him in bed with another man. I gag every time I think about it. But it was like alcohol became my new best friend.

Months have gone by, and I still don't have enough energy to sit down and talk to Anthony. I mean, what to tell him? He ruined our family, but I know I need to get over this for my kids' sake. They need and miss their daddy, but I don't believe we would ever be one again.

Chapter 3: Ryan

What's up, Ryan? A voice yelled from behind me. Oh, what's up big Mike! What's going on nothing cooling, Mike's says. What you're about to get into Ryan? I haven't talked to you in a while. Nothing I got a date with this Lil shorty in a few. Who Ashley? Mike says... man no, you know me, and that girl got an open relationship. I thought you stopped all that bullshitting and got married.

She works too damn much for me, bro. I get no kind of love or affection. You see, me and Ashley we've been together for a long time now. On and off again, we decided to have an open relationship a year ago. Though it hurts me to see her what other men, I can't see myself without her, she's a damn workaholic barely have time for me. But I can't see myself without her. Maybe I'll meet someone who would steal my heart and take me away from this hurt. "Man, you sound like a bitch, Mike said laughing.

So, who is this Lil thing you going out with? Mike asked. I don't know shorty my girl Angela set this up. Angela?! Mike said surprised, "who is this friend what her name is? I think, Katie," why? What's up. Man, we are talking about the same

Katie. If so, that's my Lil bro Karmen baby mama... Mike shouted! Man, Mike which Lil bro? You know you got too many, and he better be bloodline. Yeah bro that's bloodline, my dads' son and I don't think he's going to like this.

Are they together or something? I asked. No, he's married to another woman! Then say no more I cut him off she's not off-limits. So, I'm going to holler at you later. I got to go pick shorty up. I jumped in my car and dipped. I don't know what's wrong with this fool. I said to myself as I was driving to the location Katie gave me.

How are you doing? You've got to be Ryan; a soft sexy voice whispered to me as I got out my car. Yes, I am beautiful, and you must be Katie. Come on, let's get our seats. Table for two I said to the host, right this way! Please have a seat your server will be with ya'll shortly.

So, Katie, tell me more about yourself. I mean besides the fact that you're beautiful and Angela already mentioned that. Well she said with a smirk I'm a single mother of one, and I love reading books. My favorite author is Carl Webber. I'm a real laid-back chick if I'm not spending time with my son, I'm working. Are you not a workaholic I asked? I mean you would have time for me. I believe people make time for who they want! She said to me. So, if I like you, then you get the time.

I like how that sound. But speaking of your son, your son's father name is Karmen? Yes, why you asked that? She said with an attitude! No No, I didn't mean any harm when I asked. My homie Big Mike. "big Mike "she shouted that's Karmen's brother.

I can't stand his ass, so you mean to tell me you know Karmen? No baby just his brother. Is there anything else you need to say to me because one thing about me I don't like secrets she said in a mad voice. I don't believe, so I said well there is one little thing I know you and Angela are close and I have to be straight forward. Angela and I hooked up, and no, it's not what you're thinking. Oh, hell, no! Angela didn't mention all this shit to me I'm not even hungry no more! I have to go! Wait! Katie, she stormed off, what did I do? I'm never going to live this up; I'm glad I didn't mention Ashley.

Chapter 4: Katie

So, what's this I hear you going out on a date with ole boy? Who is oh, boy? I said to Karmen, rolling my eyes! You know damn well who oh boy is don't play stupid Katie! And I'm pretty sure you know who the ole boy is too, I said to him.

Look, Carmen, I don't have to answer to you, nor do I feel the need to. Besides, I know your lame as a brother told you. Don't play with my brother, and yeah, he told me you went out with Ryan clown ass!

Oh, so we are calling names now Carmen. Is it right or not, Katie? That's all I'm asking. Yes, and for all I know, he said he doesn't know you. Yeah, my brother said he played stupid like my name didn't ring a bell. Oh yeah but he knows we will have our day Karmen said pissed.

Look, Karmen! I'm your baby mother. I'm not your wife, nor girlfriend, I'm nothing. So, stop trying to ruin my life. You did that a year ago when you left me for that tramp so find your cake and ice cream somewhere else.

Before I knew it, I hit the ground! Karma smacked me so hard I couldn't believe it. You son of a bitch!

He grabbed me and threw me to the wall. Shut up, he yelled! you belong to me and only me until I'm finished with you. Daddy what are you doing?! Jr said; as he walked in the living room. Oh, nothing son me and your mother just clowning around. Get your stuff ready for the weekend. I'll meet you at the car.

As they left the house I fell to my knees! I can't believe he really hit me, and I let him. I'm just so confused I never seen him so angry.

Then there was a sudden knock on my door, I didn't want nobody to see me like this, so I didn't answer. But somehow the door opened. Katie! A voice screamed. I know you're in their Carmen! Wack-ass just left, and your car is in front the door. It was Angela she ran to my side as she saw me on my knees.

What's wrong hunny? He hit me he really hit me! No the hell he didn't! She said as she walked towards the door. Where are you going? Grab your bag let's go! Wait Ang! I screamed but she didn't answer. I ran behind her then jumped in her car. Put Jr location in your phone. He got some goddamn nerves to put his hands on you, the mother of his child; and Jr was in the house!

Jr didn't see nothing I said and that make it even better?! You don't let no man put their hands on you. Katie you should have picked up something and beat the hell out him with it. Now put the location on she said with a madly voice. Please stop it Ang! I've been through enough today and yesterday alone. I'm going to tell you something Katie, and I'm going to tell you this only once. Know your values, you let him hit you and not do nothing. That gives him the only option to do it again. I know you better than that. Don't never let him put his hands on you ever again. Trust me I will check that nigga when I see him. I'm not going to house wipe your tears.

Chapter 5: Angela

Hello Tracy girl meet me at my house ASAP. we have a problem, she said okay and hung up the phone. You see Tracy is our ride or die. Me and Katie knew her for 10 years now, and we all became the best of friends.

I pulled up to my house and saw Katie and to my surprise Anthony! What the hell is this fool doing here. I said to myself. I was already war ready.

What do your gay ass want and what are you doing lollygagging with him Katie. Girl calm down. Katie said with a big bruise on her face. Damn! He Hit you that hard? She hurries up and put her hand over her face. Who hit you, Anthony, said acting as he was pissed, all you be quiet and what do you want; I said to him?

I want to see my kids; they are not here Anthony. Well can we talk. As you can see, I don't have the time or the patients to speak to you right now. Come on Ang; he said with a sad face. Look Anthony we can talk later. Right now, I have to deal with this.

All I can hear was tires burning rubber. It was Tracy hitting the corner. She jumped out the car and yelled what's going on? Who I got to deal with?! She looked at Anthony, oh it's you. I grabbed her before she could launch at him. Chill out girl, and what's wrong with your damn face?!

She pushed me to the side and grabbed Katie. Carmen had beat her ass ! He did not beat me Katie said. He just hit me. Same thing I told her.

Then Anthony jumped in; he hits you where that nigga at? Just go home Anthony. I'll talk to you later. Once in his life he finally listened and got in his car and drove off.

You got to stop being so hard on him Katie said as she held her face. If you would have been harder on Carmen, your face wouldn't be looking the way it's looking. Besides, whose side are you on anyway? You were the main one saying he hurt me. Look Angela, Katie said I'm not about to keep on letting you let your anger get the best of you and keep talking crazy. You're starting to piss me off.

Okay you guys, Tracy said cut it out. No Katie said. I'm about tired of this bitch. First you act like you are trying to help me with Carmen; all while assaulting me in the process. So, you know what Angela, kiss my ass. I'm sick of being there for you, and you try to pretend to be there for me. you tear me down.

Katie got in her car and drove off. Okay what the hell just happened here. Tracy looking all confused! I don't know I said she got some damn nerves.

Well, Angela Tracy leave me alone and get the hell out of here. I said to Tracy before I could even finish my sentence. You asked me to come over. And now I'm asking you to leave. I walked in my house and slammed the door. Nothing is going right I cried out to Jesus.

I lost my husband for infidelity in which sometimes I just blame myself. Katie now hates me. What else can go wrong!

Then there was a sudden knock on my door. It was the police! Oh Lord I screamed! I then opened the door. How may I help you two officers? I was in shock; because there was my ten-year-old son standing next to the cop.

What's going on, is this your son? Yes, that's Anthony Junior. Well ma'am, he was caught stealing today. Stealing? My boy has no reason to take nothing. Ma'am we found him and his friend in which we bought him home already. The store won't press charges on them, but they are banned from the store. Without an adult he should be fortunate, now have a beautiful day the officer said walking off. Get your ass in this house Anthony and where the hell is my mother; I yelled!

Chapter 6: Ryan

Angela, I yelled from across the parking lot. She stopped. What do you want Ryan, haven't you caused enough problems? What do you mean I said? Didn't you tell Katie about me and you. Man, that wasn't about nothing. I just wanted to be real with her. Well, you were just a little too real.

Now what do you want she said angrily! Man, I heard what happened to Katie. Is that what you wanted? she said. She then walked off. I thought that was your girl. I yelled to her as she gave me the finger. What the hell is wrong with her. I said to myself.

Who was that Ryan? I jumped, bae don't do that, it was Ashley. What, I scared you? No, I'm just saying, you're just saying what Ryan? Who the hell was that? Man, that was just an old friend that you need not to worry about.

Remember open relationships! Come on say it with me. Go to hell Ryan! She said as she got in the car. Join me, I whispered. We argued the whole ride home.

I pulled in the driveway, and I yelled at her to get out. Where the hell do you think you're going? Far away from you, now shut my door! She slammed it! I don't know what's wrong with her because she's the one wanted this damn open relationship.

I really need to see what's going on with Angela. I then passed by her home and was so glad to see her car in the driveway. I knocked on her door and she opened it at one knock. What the hell do you want? Damn, calm down! I was just trying to see what ups with you and why you're acting like a 5-year-old. Who the hell you think you're talking too? Ryan!! Angel, baby calm down! Okay she said calmly.

What do you want Ryan? Don't you think you did enough? What do you mean I said confused? Did you have to tell Katie about our little fling! I mean it was nothing. Look Angela, I just want to be straight up with her. Yeah right Ryan! You act like you all was about to get married or something. You should have saved that shit for the honeymoon. I laughed! You are crazy girl.

Let me come in it look like you are going through something. No thanks Ryan, just go! Come on and let me in. She gave in and said come in but you're not staying long.

She let me in. So what's going on? The last time I told you something we ended up having sex! That don't seem like a bad idea. Ryan, she said, don't blow me. I'm just kidding. Stop being so uptight! Just open up to me. You know I'm always there for you. It is just a lot as she began to shed tears down her face.

Angela, I haven't seen you like this since that incident happened with your husband. Well is it something with him again? She said. He came over to talk but what he was talking about I did not want to hear. He's still going to be with that man! It's like everything that we had was built on a lie. I feel as though he used me just to cover up the fact that he was gay! Not only am I hurting for myself, but for my kids.

He wants to tell them the truth and still be in their life. But, I just can't! I moved closer to her. Come here, I'm sorry you have to go through this. I'm really lost for words. I know you're hurting. Before I was able to finish, she leaned in and kissed me. What are you doing, what you don't want this Angela? I'm not saying that, but I don't want to take advantage of you. You're hurt right now. Come on Ryan, make love to me like you did before. Make me forget about the pain I'm going through right now. Damn, man how can I turn it down. I mean she's beautiful and sexy. I just can't so I grabbed her and kissed her body.

I took off her clothes and I slowly made love to her. I can hear her whispers; don't stop keep going, you like that huh. I said to her, yes Ryan yes! I don't know what I just did I mean she is everything that I want Ashley to be. I thought I would never find a woman that would ever take Ashley's' place. I've been so weak behind Ashley. Then my phone rung, it was her. I got to go. Please don't leave me Angela said. I couldn't resist so I cuddled with her until she felt asleep. I put a blanket over her and ran out the door! Ashley's going to kill me I thought as I raced home.

Chapter 7: Katie

Why can't you just let me be, I said to Karmen as he pushed me to the wall! I never saw Karmen act like this. It was like he was a whole different person. It's been too long for me and you. It's time for you to give it up. You are sick! Let me go Karmen!

Oh, so it's all good when Ryan was trying to knock you off. We just went on one date and you are delusional. He gripped me tighter! Let my mommy go a little voice said from behind. It was Jr, I thought you said he was by your mom. Karmen said as he quickly let me go.

You see, Jr didn't want to go over there. He begged me and he cried. I knew something had to be wrong because Jr loves going by his father. I lied Karmen, now please just leave! I'm not going nowhere without my son. He then grabbed him by the back of his neck. He told him to go get his stuff.

Daddy you're hurting me, stop it! Let him go! I yelled at the top of my lungs! He let loose of Jr just to smack me to the ground! I was so furious; I didn't know what to do so I got up and I ran to my room. I grabbed my shoebox from on top of my closet and grabbed my gun! I then ran back to the living room let him go!

I shot one round and the bullet from the gun hit my lamp instead of his leg. Which I was aiming for! You crazy bitch, put that gun away. No, not until you leave my house. Mommy I'm scared, said Jr.. don't worry baby, daddy is about to leave, isn't you Karmen! Karmen said you are lucky you have that gun in your hand, as he walked out the front door. Just to sit in his car in front of my door.

Twenty minutes had passed and he was still sitting out in front my door! What is this fool doing! I said to myself as I peeked out of the window. Suddenly a police car pulled up and there was a knock on my door.

Please open the door! Yes officer, I said. How may I help you? The officer then said; I was told by this gentleman right here that you're not cooperating with court order. What do you mean, I said? It is his weekend with the boy, so you have to let him go ma'am! You can't let my son go with him, he doesn't want to go, he is scared of him! I'm sorry there's nothing I can do about that; the police said to me. You would have to check with the courts Monday and file a complaint. Until then, you have to release the boy. Karmen stared at me with an evil look and smirk on his face. This is not over Karmen; I will get you for this.

The officer said, please ma'am don't make any threats. I rolled my eyes and said I'm sorry Jr baby. But every chance you get to go to Daddy's house, please call Mommy. Please don't make me go, he yelled as he wiped his tears! Boy get in the car! Karmen yelled.

How does this make you feel Karmen? Your son doesn't want to go with you, shut up bitch. I'm not finished with you yet! Okay you all cut it out, the police said. Now you have your son now, go ahead and get out of here, the officer said. Can you let this less than a man better, yet sperm donor know he better have my son home on time Sunday evening. You heard that sir; the officer said. Yeah yeah yeah, Karmen said as he walked away and put his hands up. I slammed my front door! I can't believe him. I don't know what's going on in that head of his, but Karmen must be stopped.

Chapter 8: Angela

I can't believe I let you come over. Well, we need to talk Angela, Anthony said. Okay talk then. Angela you got to hear me out, I never meant to hurt you. I never thought in a million years we would be at this point in our life's, and I can't believe you cheated on me with a man! A damn man Anthony! You know how many diseases they got going on around here.

How long has this been going on Anthony and don't lie to me? Come on Angela. Don't come on Angela shit. You're going to tell me everything I want to know, or you could get up and leave now. Baby I don't think you can handle the truth. Try me! Okay Anthony said as he took a deep breath.

I always have been gay. I just was afraid to come out when I met you years back. I just knew you would be the one to change me, and when we had our first child together. I thought maybe just maybe I could get over this fetish for men. Then suddenly, I met Maurice and that changed.

You sick fuck! So you mean to tell me you been seeing him for 6 years now? You mean to tell me that you met him after we had our first child! You have to understand Angela, that I've been like this since I was a child. I always felt like I was different. I always had the attraction for men.

I cried and said; why be with me then Anthony? Why have three kids for me! Why not just come out! I broke down in tears. I'm sorry Angela, I'm so sorry! I never meant to hurt you. I never did, but I was a sucker for you. I made myself love you, until I felt in love with you! I did and I still do. You don't love me, if you loved me you would have left me where I was. But instead, you married me and had kids with me. Then you betrayed me and put a knife in my back!

Why don't you just finish me, you don't know what I went through growing up. Angela, I barely had friends. My mom and dad turned their backs on me because I was different. I love the opposite sex.

Wait, so it's obvious I was just a game to you! I meant nothing since day one. It is also obvious your family knew too. I'm sorry I'll say said it over and over again.

Maurice and I want to make this right. You and Maurice you got to be kidding me. I'm serious Angela, it's time for me to stop lying to myself and others. Especially you and the kids, it's time for me to live my life how it should have been lived.

I love you Angela, but I want to live my life as a gay man. I then screamed at Anthony! You won't be doing that around my kids either faget.

Hey, watch your mouth Angela. Please don't tell me what to do faget. Now get out! I tried to come here and talk to you like an adult. But you don't want to hear me out. So, I'll see you in court Angela.

Chapter 9: Katie

Is someone sitting here? A voice from behind me said. I turned around and looked and this tall caramel complexion, handsome man was standing behind me.

I began to stutter a little as he smiled and sat down. How are you doing beautiful; he said to me. I blushed so hard, then said I'm doing fine and yourself. Hey, I can't complain I'm living. I see you are reading a book. What are you reading? A book called "Something on the Side by Carl Weber. Oh, I hear he have some great books. Yes, he does I said.

Do you mind if I ask; are you single? I looked at him and said yes I am! But as I can see you're not, as he looked down at his ring finger. Yeah, my wife passed away 2 years ago, and I never found that special someone that can make me get rid of it. I said I'm sorry to hear that, but can I get your name?

We both laughed! I'm sorry, my name is Quincy, but people call me Q for short. Awesome and I'm Katie, just call me Katie. Well Katie, tell me a little more about yourself if you don't mind, he said. No, I don't. I'm an RN at the local hospital.

You save lives, he said to me as he looked me in my eyes. Save mines, I laughed. I see you're funny!

But anyways, I have one son. Do you have any kids? Yes, a son he's seven. Oh, that's good. My son is six. So, your son's father; why you not with him. I said that's a long and embarrassing story. I need not to explain that situation that's cool baby. I understand.

Maybe one day you can open up to me. What you mean about one day? I mean, I'm going to leave you my number and if you call me that means I have a second date with you. Okay, now he sounds crazy. Like where did we go on our first date. This is just the beginning he got up left his number and walked off.

Now if that didn't just turn me on, I don't know what did. I grabbed my purse and ran to my car. The phone rang, and it was Karmen he lucky he has Jr are else I would ignore his ass hello, hey Katie can we talk about? I want to apologize; ok I accept goodbye. No Katie for real can we meet up at our favorite spot? Hmmm you mean I use to be favored. The same thing Kat look, Karmen, I'm not for your bullshit, not today. I'm serious come on, you're lucky I'm down the street I hung up. If this nigga tries me, I have my mace, and I'm loaded. I'm listening; I said as I walked up to him. I'm so glad you came. Yeah ok, I'm here what's up and where is jr? Oh, he's with my mom. Look I'm sorry I never meant to hurt you when I found out you went on a date with Ryan clown ass. That had me pissed. But why your married I said rolling my eyes, to be honest, I always thought I had you wrapped around my fingers I mean to be fair he said how many men you talk to after we split, carmen is kind of right it was like when he left me my whole world fell apart but still no reason. So, you thought I was going to play side chick? No, not at all. I miss our family ties. Well, Karmen, don't you think you're a year too late.

It's never too late for Love Karmen said to me, well it's too late for my love I'm over you and all the drama , you don't mean that Katie Karmen yes I do and why you're not home with your pregnant wife instead worrying about me, that's the problem she's not you will never be you I messed up how can I fix this , you can't I said to Karmen and walked off he ran behind me and grab me. Back off Karmen, I'm sorry Katie. I can't picture my life without you he said as he pulled me in tightly to him. Well your timing is all fucked up. I kicked him in the private area and pepper sprayed him as he yelled. I ran as fast as I could. Got in my car and drove off. The next few days I was just moping around the house with nothing to do and a lot on my mind. I couldn't call Angela because I'm still pissed at her then I doubt if she wanted to talk anyway.

Jr was with Karmen ass and I hated that, and Jr did also the way he calls every hour wishing he could come home, ummm what should I do today I said to myself.

Then a light bulb went off in my head duhh Katie call Quincy or should I say Q. Now where did I put my phone. I saved his number in my phone that night I just knew I would be calling him one of these good ole days. The phone rung he answered.

Hello, Quincy, speaking, damn I said to myself he sounds sexier over the phone. Hello Quincy, repeated himself, oh hey Q this is Katie you know the one he jumped in and said I know who you are. I blushed oh so you do. Yup! I'm still waiting on our second date I laughed. You are crazy. I could be at times, he said. But anyway, how are you doing. I'm doing good I wasn't expecting to hear from you, and why is that. You look stuck up he said. Stuck up, I laughed you don't know me. I'm far from that. Well, Katie, I have a business call on the other line, but before I go I would like to take you out on that second date you know a real one this time, I think I would like that I said smiling to myself ok love bug I call you a little bit later.

Chapter 10: Angela

Last night was beautiful. I said to Ryan. He left me asleep only to call me and tell me that he ran out of gas. I bought him back to my place where we fell asleep. Yes, Angela, he said. It was, but Ashley is going to kill me. I didn't even come home last night, and I didn't realize you really lied to me. I told him I would never try to hook Katie up with you remember. I have a wife, and we both agreed to an open relationship. What kind of shit is that I said to Ryan?

I was on the verge of losing her, and I didn't want to let go. You're so weak I said to him, says the woman whose husbands left her for a man. I smacked him his face! How dare you! I'm sorry, but what did you expect? I grew up with homie. He acted and looked gay. I don't see how you couldn't see that. Ray Charles, he laughed oh, so you think this is funny now. No, I don't.

There was a sudden knock on my door. Who's that Angela, I don't know I'm not expecting anybody this morning. I went to the door and looked out the peephole. It was Anthony. I swung the door open what do you want I came here to talk Angela I'm not for your bullshit today he pushed open my door who is this in my house? You're home. Anthony, you have some nerves. He forced me to the side. I know that is not that nigga Ryan. What's up with It Ryan, said to Anthony. Don't know what up me what you are doing in my house, man don't come at me. I'm here for your wife. Look Anthony, I don't know what you want but as you can you see I have company. Can you leave, so you're telling me you're screwing my wife. Soon to be ex-wife you fag. Bitch don't play with me, bitch!!?

Who you are calling a! Before I could finish my sentence, Anthony and Ryan went to rumbling. You guys cut It out, don't you ever disrespect her like that Ryan said. He consistently punches Anthony in his face. Cut it out Ryan before you kill him! Ryan let loose and Anthony dropped to the ground. I can't believe Ryan took action like that.

He really turns me on I just wanted to rip all of his clothes off him and do you know what to him. You see Anthony never been manly to me that's why I'm kind of surprised he even step to Ryan like that.

Thinking about it Ryan had some gayish ways, and I always overlooked it because I loved that clown. I wish I never met him yet alone had kids for him. Okay you all enough with this madness I think you both should leave this is my house. Angela I'm not going anywhere. You know what Anthony; I'm done arguing with you. You played me like a fool had everybody laughing and giggling talking about me. I went through so much with you sleepless nights.

Being away from my babies for months. I even lost my best friend because of the anger I have for you. I took it out on her, Angela imma go Ryan said. It seems like y'all need to talk. Yes, get out Anthony said.

We're both going you can have this fucking house. Nothing but old memories of you and me. I want to wash that away I'm so over you. It isn't even funny. I began to walk out of the house. Come on, Ryan just a sec Anthony said. I wanted this to be between you and me, but it's obvious you are fucking him. You and Mister Sucker Punch might want to go to the doctor so you all can get a check-up. Why is that I said looking confused. Because I found out yesterday, I could have HIV. Ryan fell to the ground, while I stand there looking with my mouth open. Anthony walked off smoothly. Close your mouth he said, as he walked out the front door. He said to Ryan you can keep that piece of shit I had no words to say I was in shock, and so was Ryan.

Chapter 11: Ryan

It's been a long three days since I talked to Angela. She's been calling my phone and I haven't been answering. it's so much to deal with. How did I get myself involved with this bullshit? I've been hurting myself all this time allowing myself to have an open relationship with Ashley knowing what all that comes with it. I mean come on just think about it. She has multiple sex partners and so does I. I screwed up, I'm embarrassed and ashamed of myself. I just can't stop thinking about this situation.

Hey babe, what's going on, Ashley said. She walked in the room, hey honey we need to talk. You see when I made it back home to Ashley. I made up with her and apologized. I told her that I didn't want to do this open relationship anymore. Seemed like I was scared straight. She didn't totally agree with it, but we did decide to not see anybody else for the time being.

What you want to talk about baby? I don't know how I'm going to tell Ashley about this, but I didn't have the courage to say it to her that day. But I know I need to for our safety. Its either now or never. I don't know how to tell you this come here sit next to me.

What is it Ryan baby! I never saw you like this she said to me baby. Please promise me you won't leave me what's wrong? She yelled I messed up I mean I fucked up. I think we need to get checked! What are you talking about she said with a confused look on her face? What you got something? That's the problem I don't know, we may have HIV. She stood up so fast; what the hell you are talking about HIV!

I don't know how to explain this well you better get the fuck to explaining. Baby calm down stop cussing, calm down Ryan? You are going to tell me to calm down when you just said we might have HIV. What bitch you was going in raw. Look, Ashley, I don't think me telling you who it is going to solve anything. Ryan Williams, you better look me in my face and tell me who this bitch is. Oh, I get it someone caught feelings, no actually that's not the reason. I don't want to cause any more drama. I want to get tested Ryan she said with a high-pitched voice!

Okay Ashley since you consent, you damn right I do. Just calm down and let me explain Ryan. Don't tell me to calm down. Okay, Ashley remember we were in in the parking lot and you walked up on me talking to a female. What they got to do with it. Well that was her. Apparently, her husband is gay. He caught me by her house we fought and all, so you are telling me you're fighting behind bitch now. What happened to just walk away. You got me at home.

Remember Ryan are you just all in your damn feelings she interrupts me saying. You know what Ashley this is all your fault. Anyway, I've been telling you I want to stop this open relationship bullshit. I want to just be with you. You know you want to have your fun an you're a workaholic at the same damn time.

I've been acting like a little bitch for you for the past years and yeah, I caught feelings for her and I'm sure you caught feelings for one of them lying ass Dudes you were messing with.

Oh hell no. You're not about to switch everything off on me and think it's my fault you're the one sleeping with the bitch of the faget you know what Ashley, I'm done. I'm over your ass you made my life a living hell since I agreed to this crazy-ass open relationship. You know we could have caught plenty diseases at the rate we were going. You know where you screwed up at, what you mean screwed up? I never messed with another man. The only reason why I agreed and wanted this open relationship is so I can still have you in the house paying all the damn bills, while I stack my money up like the workaholic that you say IAM. So, I can leave your sorry ass, and now you messed my life up by telling me this bullshit that I might have HIV. I should have been left your ass a long time ago. You ruined my life you better hope I don't have that shit cause I'ma light fire to that ass. You can't be serious I'm dead serious Ryan now let's get tested, go by your damn self I grabbed my keys and left.

Chapter 12: Katie

I never laughed this hard before. I said to Quincy. You really have a way with words. Well you know I am not trying to be cocky, but I know a little something huh. I blushed. I just know how to treat a woman. You're a black queen you're beautiful and by the way you talk like you're brilliant. Well thank you for the compliments. I'm very flattered.

Mom! Junior ran up to us with Quincy's son Quin. We need more tokens. "We decided to take the kids out on our second date. I really didn't know whether to agree with it because I didn't want anybody to meet my son so fast. Quincy seem like the most down to earth gentleman I ever met before in my life. Yeah, I said Life. It just seems so unreal to me.

I mean he's treated me with the most respect, he always texting me good morning and goodnight making sure I'm okay. Am I hungry, and you know that's the way to a woman's heart. Just fill me up with food. I laughed to myself.

Mom, okay you guys can take some more money... hold on bae. Did you just call me bae? I said to myself, you guys take 20 a piece Quincy said go finish playing and come back in about 15 minutes the food should be ready. Okay Dad, Quin said. Thank you, Mr., Then they both ran off.

What's up Katie, I looked up and it was Karmen wife! Oh, hey Tasha, where is Junior? Oh, I'm sorry my name is Tasha, she said to Quincy. I'm Junior's stepmom" how you doing he said to her, I pray Karmen isn't here. He going to ruin my date.

I wonder does she know how he keep on throwing himself at me. Hitting me then again as I looked in her face her eyes were kind of dark like she had a black eye. I hope he wasn't beating on this girl she's pregnant I said to myself. Well you know Karmen is outside getting the kids out of the car. If Jr is here, I know he would love to see him. I bet he would I mumbled. What was that? Tasha said oh nothing, we were just about to leave.

But we haven't... Quincy said, but I quickly interrupted him. Yep we're about to go. I grabbed the kids and quickly ran outside the door. We got in the car and I knew Quincy was staring at me. Look I know you are wondering what's going on or what that was about, but that's a long story and I don't think the kids need to be listening to this conversation. I understand Katie, let's just get some McDonald's and head back to the house.

Man, we were having fun the kids said. I hope we do it again. Trust me, there will be plenty more fun dates Quincy said. Oh my God! This man is unbelievable it's like he just fell out of heaven just for me. Lord I know you heard my prayers, please don't let anything come between this blessing you sent me.

As we made it back to my house the kids went in the room to play the game. Quincy and I was in my room talking. So, since we are alone, Katie tell me why you were so bothered at Dave & Buster's. Oh my God. I don't know where to start.

So, me and Jr daddy broke up a year ago and to be honest he left me for her. The lady that we saw today. Everything was all good yeah, I still was hurting and stuff, but I was getting over it. Now since I really show no interest in him, he's making my life a living hell. I showed him the bruise on my arm… I keep it covered because he did this to me. My son doesn't want to go over there but we got a court order. He must go. I even shot at him. That's still not doing nothing. I really don't want to put you in all of this, but I feel the need to tell you. It seems like he's getting dangerous and I understand if you want to leave!

Wow slow down! That really is a lot to deal with, said Quincy. I'm sorry that you're going through this but let me tell you, I'm no coward and I see the fear in your eyes. I need you to get rid of that. I'm going to protect you, but when I'm not around I need you to protect yourself and that little boy. He's putting his hands on you makes me even madder. I don't even know the cat, but I promise you I got your back.

Lord this has got to be a joke, you did this one. I hugged him so tight, but you barely know me. Just by this short time of getting to know you I know you're a good woman. My toes started to curl and before you knew it, I leaned in and kissed him. I can't believe I did that I'm sorry, too soon.

No, I promise you it's not he leaned in and kissed me back. Oh my God I can't believe I'm about to do this. I've been celibate for so long I need this so bad his touch! His touch is so gentle, he knows just what to do. He kissed all over my body I mean every single part of it. I whisper take it, just take it already. As he slipped in my body felt a big relief, that I haven't felt in a long time. I just want to let out a big Moan! How does it feel he whispered into my ears? It feels so good I said to him. I can't believe I'm doing this is so soon. I just met him a couple of weeks ago I feel like a whore, and that was just something I was going to have to accept. Because my body needed it.

After we were done, my legs were still trembling. He wrapped his arms around me, and we fell asleep. Thank you Lord I whispered

Chapter 13: Angela

The doorbell rang. I was too drained to answer so I laid on my couch hoping whoever It was would go away! Then I heard a big boom and my door opened. Angela, I know you're in there. The voice said from the outside. Then knock on the door again.

I knew that voice from anywhere, it was Katie. I ran to the door, what are you doing here? I act like I didn't want her here. But I actually was so happy to see her. She gave me a big hug and I just broke down in tears. Its ok honey, she said to me. Just let it all out. Katie I'm so sorry, I didn't mean any of that I said. I'm sorry too Angela I got in my feeling too fast. Come in girl, your mama called me crying saying, please check up on you.

I've been losing my mind ever since that day with Anthony and Ryan. I haven't been having my kids either. My mother thought they would be safer with her and I totally agreed. You see the day after that happened, I overdosed on my pain pills. It was not on purpose. I kept telling myself that my kids found me on the ground passed out and called their grandma.

It was so horrible and that's something I would never want my kids ever to see me do again.

My mother called the police and rushed over. She beat them to my house that's how fast she was going. I just feel bad that I keep putting my mama in the situation where is like she's babysitting me all over again. I told her not to tell nobody including Katie. But it's obvious she didn't listen, and I'm glad she didn't.

So, Angela what's going on why did you try and kill yourself. She just went right into the point. Ugh Katie I missed you so much friend. I didn't have any one to go to. Who would understand my pain like you do. I thought I really lost you. Angela, our argument wasn't that deep for you to ever feel that our friendship of 20 years would be over. Katie said as she hugged me again.

You should have just called me; now talk to me I know it's dealing with Anthony. Since the last time we spoke, did y'all to ever get the chance to talk things out, Katie asked. Man, everything been a mess, brace yourself for what I'm about to tell you. I said to Katie.

I'm listening, you remember Ryan, right? Yeah girl what about him, well he came over to talk to me and like a fool I let him in. Long story short we slept together, oh wow! She said thought you had no feelings for him. I didn't, you didn't, so what changed. Katie said because I remember you trying to hook us up yeah Katie that's old let's not get into that. But Anthony came over and caught me and Ryan together and got mad.

Angela, I thought he like men now? Me too we both laughed. He was so upset that he called me out my name. Before I knew it, Ryan and Anthony were fighting! You got to be kidding me said Katie. Yes girl. They really were fighting. I told them both to leave and Anthony wanted to be cocky talking about he's not going nowhere. So, I was like you know what I'm going to leave and before I could leave, he stopped Ryan.

Looked me in my face and said you all might want to get checked with a smirk on his face. I knew it had to be something terrible girl. I'm just lost for words. I don't even know how to tell you this. Just tell me Ang. I think I might have HIV. Well that's what Anthony says.

Wait, what Katie, said loudly. Yes, you heard me right I said as tears fell down my eyes, that bastard. Stop crying you know I got you. Did you get tested yet, no I'm too scared? Katie, you have to do it baby girl. You don't want to wreck your brain wondering if you have it or not. Kate my life is all screwed up I don't even care whether I live or die at this point. Stop talking like that Katie said to me. You have three beautiful kids to think about, don't you ever say those words out your mouth again. Now we're going to go down there together, and I'll be there with you every step of the way. We're going to figure this out and I promise you. I'm so glad to have a friend like Katie she's always there for me no matter what the situation.

Chapter 14: Ryan

What a way to tell somebody that you don't love them, or never did. She was just using me up I said to my homeboy Kirk man. That's your fault, I told you to leave that stuck-up bitch alone bro. I'm hurting right now. Man, you better man the hell up. You know I don't like that weak shit around me.

I don't even know why I'm talking to Kirk he always showing that tough love he been telling me to leave Ashley. He didn't even come to our wedding. Oh girl been using you. Kirk said. but you got more significant problems right now.

I told him about the HIV virus that I may have. He's the only person I can really trust. Not to mention my business, this shit really stressing me out. I haven't been eating barely sleeping at night.

Ryan I'm about to head out. I got to go pick up my baby Mama. Keep me updated and look man stop worrying about that broad. He gave me a dap and dipped out. Shit I'm so confused I don't know what to do. But I know I don't want to do this alone. The only person I can think of was Angela.

I grabbed my keys and headed to her house. I knocked on the door and to my surprise, Katie answers the door. What's up she said, the last time I saw her was when she ran out on our date. It was kind of weird seeing her here. I mean Angela did try to hook us up.

Hey Katie, is Angela here. Come in she said, I've been trying to call you. Angela said to me sitting on the couch, I know and I'm sorry. I just been going through it with all that's been going on. You should hate me right now I don't hate you Angela. I'm mad at myself, it seems like y'all two really need to talk.

I'm going to be in the other room if you need me. Katie said to her friend. Okay Angela said. I took a seat next to her on the couch and took a deep breath. Ashley left me, I'm so sorry Ryan. I know it was about this situation we are going through right now, yeah that too, but she also added that she never did love me. She was just using me, wow why so harsh. I don't know I said, but I'm over that. You think you know someone but really don't, tell me about Angela said.

I never thought my husband would cheat on me especially with no damn man. Speaking of husbands where he at? I don't need any repeats, yeah, we both don't. But you don't have to worry about him popping up trust me.

Did you ever went got tested she asked, no how bout you she looked at me all sad, no. I've been scared, do you want to go together? I mean we are in this together. Her face brightening up, yes, I would like that. Let's go now I know a clinic that would test us for free right away.

I've been calling around, she said but was afraid to go. Can Katie come? Of course, she went to the backroom to get her, they both came out. Then we left.

The drive there was quiet, all I could think of is what if I have HIV, could I love the same. Would I even be the same? I wish I could turn back the hands of time. I would have thought smarter. I feel so dumb inside.

As we approached the clinic I started sweating. Come on you guys, Katie said it's going to be ok. Angela and me both looked at each other and said speak for yourself. She heard me and gave me an ugly look. I am, she said with an attitude and rolled her eyes. I decided to take the test with you Ang. I mean it won't hurt to check myself too, right Katie said. No, it won't Angela replied, well let's go ladies.

When we walked in everyone stopped and stared at us. Angela turned around as if she was about to leave. Where are you going, I said to her? I can't do this. Yes, you can.

How may I help you guys an old lady said from behind the counter? Yes ma'am, we are all here for an HIV TEST ok. Who would like to go first ? Me, Katie replied all fast like were not the ones in a damn crisis. Ok, come to the back with me and y'all two can fill these forms out. I'll call the next person after I finish with her ok. Thank you ma'am Angela and I both replied, are you nervous I whisper to her yes, like hell were going to get through this together I held her hand tight.

Chapter 15: Katie

It was a breezy morning. I laid in bed right on the side of my new man Quincy! I could hear the wind hit against my window as he rolled over and gave me a kiss. Good morning beautiful, I blushed as I said good morning handsome, how did you sleep? Like a baby he responded. I know you did all that snoring. He laughed and said I don't snore. I said next time I'm recording your butt. Ok bet beautiful.

I guess I'll start getting breakfast ready for us. Oh, you were because I was about to finish my dinner from last night. Oh, you were? I said biting my bottom lip. He knows that turns me on when he talks nasty like that.

Tell me Quincy what do you see in me besides sex. Don't get me wrong the shit be amazing I said with a smirk. But I got to know are we in this for long term? I feel where you're coming from, he said. But trust me I'm here for the long term. I'm not here to play with your feelings. I'm trying to be that better man for you that you've been looking for a long time. I'm here for it beautiful. I love it when you call me beautiful, makes me feel good about myself. Also, knowing I have a man that reminds me every day that I am beautiful. Baby you are beautiful. I tell you that because I mean that shit. You should feel that way rather I say it or not. There's nothing like a beautiful black queen.

But when we have these men that want to take our Queens down like your son father did, its harder for a man like me to build you back up. I could look you in your eyes and could tell that you're still hurting. Baby he didn't deserve your love. Now I'm here to pick up the pieces that another man broke. I'm up for the challenge trust and believe me.

Damn Quincy, that was deep. But while he was saying all that my mind drifted away thinking about Angela an what's she's going through. What's wrong beautiful I flinch, oh I'm sorry baby. Tell me what is on your mind. I hope it was me.

It was Quincy I smiled and leaned in to give him a kiss, but he pushed back, not until you tell me what's bothering you. I can feel something wrong. Ugh ok I took a deep breath. My girlfriend Angela the one I was telling about, yes ok. What about her? I know you was upset with her and like I told you life is too short. Yes, I know you told me that.

So anyways her mama called me and said she tried to kill herself. Damn Quincy said and why was that? she's going through so much I started to cry, and I feel bad. I wasn't there like I have always been there for her since day one. Dry your eyes and stop your crying. You can't fight every battle. Sometimes God separate people for a reason. Some long term and others like you and your friend short terms to test y'all strength.

I'm sure she doesn't hate you or nothing. I wiped my tears. No, she doesn't. It just hurts to know what's she's going through. But trust me beautiful, God put his toughest battles on his strongest people. You and I are an example.

I've lost my wife I thought life was over for me. then you came along and gave me strength to go on. When I saw you sitting there alone, I thought to myself she got to be mines. Before he could continue there was a big bang at my door.

Who the hell knocking on my door at this time of the morning? Bang, bang, bang that's all I heard. I opened the door and to my surprise its Karmen. What the hell is your problem? He swung my door open. Where is my son Katie? I'm not here to talk. He's in the room. Well he text me to come and get him. I know you're lying. No, he isn't mama. I want to go by my daddy. Wow! I thought to myself. You had a change of heart just a week ago. He couldn't stand his daddy. But I would not stand in way if he really wants to go.

Ok baby get your stuff. Back to you, don't come banging on my door this time of the morning. I have company, man fuck you and your company. Excuse me Quincy, said walking out of my bedroom.

Who the hell is this clown Katie? I hope this isn't the dude my son talking about. What are you talking about Jr, I yelled? Mom I'm right here. What are you telling you father? I don't want to talk about it. He walked out of the front door with his head down. You got to be kidding me. Man, all I know is you better keep that clown away from my son or else. Or else what, Quincy quickly respond.

Karmen stepped to Quincy as if he was going to hit him. Y'all chill out I screamed! Karmen have him back by Monday or I will call the cops. Yeah whatever Karmen said as he walked out the door. I don't know what's his problem nor Jr. I said to myself.

I mean what could Quincy so called possibly tell my son to make him want to go by his daddy! I'm not about to be putting up with this bullshit you hear me Katie. I looked at him with a crazy look on my face. Now who the hell he talking to. Put up with what? When a father is concerned about his son. You know what I mean Katie, yeah, I do but the bigger problem. What did your son tell my son? I don't know Katie. But I will have a talk with him. Yeah you just do that. Where is he anyway? With all this commotion going on.

I thought to myself but didn't ask. Everything went left just that fast. I mean me and him went from having a beautiful conversation, to this. Carmen always ruining shit. Or maybe I'm a Sucker for Love once again. Katie, we need to talk. About this relationship Quincy said. I am falling in love with you just that quick. You did? yes, I did, and I think we should elope and get married what you think? Marriage? I said to him. I think he's the Sucker, Quincy were both no ready for that it's too soon, nothing never too soon beautiful think about it.

Chapter 16: Angela

When my test results came back negative, I really had a big weight lifted off my shoulder. I still seemed to be unhappy. Especially with all that went on these last couple of months. My husband, my soulmate how could someone who took a vow do me so dirty. Thinking about our past we were so in love so happy at least I thought I will never love the same.

I decided to let Anthony and his new man, yes man. I still can't believe this shit. My eyes started to water, but they supposed to be stopping by. I need some kind of closure. I can't keep him away from his kids. They need him more than ever. And to break my heart even more Ryan decided to go back to his wife after the test results can back negative.

Yes, after he told me how she did him he ran back. That is a weak nigga, but I can't be mad at him. I was stupid for even sleeping with a married man over and over again. Hoping maybe just maybe I could have a chance at his heart. But at the end of the day he belongs to someone else.

Then there was a knock on my door. I jumped up bracing myself knowing that could be Anthony. I open the door, but it was a woman, yes may I help you. Angela right? The women replied , yes and you are? My name is Ashley, I'm Ryan's wife. I'ma make this quick and simple stay the hell away from my man. I don't know what you thought y'all had but he's mines. I know this bitch is joking I said to myself. Look honey you can have him. No, you look honey she rudely interrupted I GOT HIM. Her voice got a lil higher and I'm pregnant, so like I said stay away far away.

How did this troll looking bitch get my address? you know what I'm not about to go back and forward with you, I'm over everything right now. I said to myself, I simply replied with an ok and shut the door in her face. You just didn't know how bad I wanted to pull that tramp in my house a whoop her ass. But at the end of the day that is her husband.

There was another knock on the door I quickly opened it and yelled, didn't I tell you okay! Thinking it was still her. But it was Anthony. He replied are you ok? I'm sorry, thought you were someone else. Come in and where is your boo I said being sarcastic. He's in the car. I want to make sure you're really ok with this. Yes, Anthony, that's why I invited you all over.

He waved at the car, and a white man got out of the car. You got to be fucking kidding me Anthony not only is he a man, he's a white man? Yes, Angela don't be so judgmental. You should have said that before your ass cheated. Chill out he's coming.

How are you doing I'm Marcus he said in the gayest voice ever. Angela, I said and walked in the house. They followed. Ok well Anthony told me so much about you and the kids. Oh, he did can't be all good he left us for you. Stop it Angela I left you not my kids, oh so that's how your coming, I'm just honest. Oh, ok so since we're honest, if I would have never caught you cheating would you kept playing both sides. No, Angela I was going to tell you, but I was waiting on the right time.

Yeah whatever so how did you guys meet? I mean it's obvious he is not the same guy you were cheating on me with. Yes, we also were going thru some things, Marcus replied. His voice urks my nerves. Oh ok so you forgive him I'm guessing? Yes, he told me everything. Of course, I'm in love with him also. It was one time, but just how you found him married, is the same way you might lose him. ever thought of that I asked, we didn't come her for no consulting Anthony said. He was aggravated, who said you did. Well let's move on, Angela.

I apologize to you I know your hurting, and I admit I was wrong. I did you wrong, but you got to let that hurt go. Anthony, I don't want to her all that. I know I will move on, and it will all get better in time. I'm a strong woman. Though I went through a breakdown, God will see me through. This, too, shall pass. I wish you guys, or should I say gals the best of luck, I forgive you. Only for our kids' sake. They need you right now, and they miss you dearly. What you got going on is not my problem anymore, thank you Angela that's all I wanted to hear is you forgive me. So, I decided to give you the house so you and the kids could still have their rooms.

I cut him off no Anthony I'm moving out; you see this house was given to Anthony by his late grandma and I don't want it anymore. Too many old memories. Are you sure Angela I mean you can keep it , it's yours I will sign it over to you , I'm positive, Life has brought me pain and joy my husband left me for a man, my best friend and I felt out due to my anger but were still standing strong .I fell for a man that I thought wanted me as I wanted him. I just feel so used up. I was a Sucker for love to men that didn't deserve my Love. It is time for me to focus on me and my happiness and my kids' happiness. Being a Sucker for love taught me a lot about love and I'm over it all.

Chapter 17: Ryan

Ashely did that make any sense; did we really have to go to her house. Yes, we did, and your scary ass should have gotten out the car and addressed her. You should have let her know we're serious. I already told her, she knows me, and you are back together. Why are you so upset Ryan? Ashely ask, it's just you be doing too much first I agree to have an open relationship with you just to keep what we have alive. Then you tell me you don't love me and never did. I don't know what to believe, you know I was lying. Ryan baby and now that I'm pregnant with our first child, things are really about to change. No more open relationship, but didn't you say you were never sleeping with anyone anyway. That doesn't matter anymore Ryan, yes it does Ashley.

How I'm I supposed to know if that's really my baby? Shit we barely slept together. What are you trying to say Ryan? You know exactly what I'm saying. You see I don't trust her ass when my homie was telling me all that shit about her makes me think. I know bro wouldn't lie to me, you know what Ryan, I can't do this every time I think we're good you make me regret coming back to your tired ass. And you make me feel like everything you said was lies Ashley. I don't trust you, and I'm not about to continue living life like this. I want a divorce. What! A divorce Ryan. You're out your damn mind, plus I'm pregnant. Ashely, I don't give a damn if that baby is mines. Then I will be there for it. I'm done with being a sucker for your love. You always been weak, Ashley said to me. Not no more let me out or walk from here.

Get out you piece of shit. I won't see you again I couldn't get out the car fast enough. Life is what you make it. I've been living a life with a person I thought truly loves me. I gave my all and it still wasn't enough though. I'll take my share of mistake; never will I again agree to an open relationship. She was right about one thing, I was weak, but I was raised to stand up for your love. I guess I was standing too tall. I lost a friend in the process Angela was the most real as it comes and I'm hurting that I put her in this love triangle she was already going through a lot already.

Now I know she wouldn't even talk to me especially with that stunt Ashley pulled. Why did I let it go that far? How could I make it right? I took my phone out and sent Angela a text, I'm sorry! I wrote that's all I could say bro you need a ride it was my friend, Kirk get in. What you are doing walking, man bro I just got into it with Ashley. Man, you still playing with that Lil girl still can't believe you married her. Yeah bro I know I am over her ass this time for good. Then she says she's pregnant, aww man. That could be anyone's baby bro, wifey was extensive. I didn't want to tell you do y'all agreement. I believe you bro I don't even wanna talk about it are here no more I received a text message it was Angela. Now that took me to be surprised, she replied with a smiling face and that was it. I wonder what's going on in her head, I got to get her back.

Chapter 18: Katie

I had to meet up with Angela at our favorite restaurant to tell her all that's going on. The Lil boy is troubled Angela girl. I had Quincy confront him about what he told Jr. The Lil boy went crazy, girl now you wonder why Jr got the hell, Angela said. He never shows any sign of having an anger problem. I mean him and Jr play so good together in the beginning. Now, they don't play at all.

Then girl you know Quincy asked me to marry Him? What you just met this guy. I know but he seems like Mr. Right, ok so what about his son. Mr. wrong, I laughed you're so crazy, but I think it have a lot to do with the passing of his mother. I think he might need some counseling. Nah Katie I think he needs an ass whooping will do the trick. Girl I can't stand you.

But on the serious note how you going to marry a man you barley know? Angela, I didn't say yes, oh good she replied, neither did I say no. She looked at me Katie you were just mesmerized, and barely getting over Carmen. Now you are talking about considering marring John doe. Wait I'm confused who is John doe, exactly yeah don't know him, he could be a serial killer, Ang he would have been killed me don't you think, hell maybe he's waiting on the right time. Angela, I yelled stop scaring me. you should be scared Katie, ok I'm not even hungry anymore. Get the bill, ok and I'm sorry Katie, I didn't mean to upset you. I just speaking possible facts I'll be right back, I got to go to the rest room, ok girl.

Lord, she's working on my nerves with all that nonsense. I said to myself now she has me wondering. Hey, do you mind if I set here. Oh, hey well my friend is sitting here but we're about to go waiting on our bill. It won't take long she said to me.

Excuse me who are you, my and is Brittany, you don't know me, but I know you. Well enlighten me, does this ring a bell, she reaches in her purse and placed a picture on my table. To my surprise it was Quincy!

I've been spying on you guys for the last couple of weeks now. He's my husband! Wait you lost me when you said husband and trust me you don't know me Ms. Brittany. Yes I do you live on Oak Drive don't you? Yes, but I'm still not understanding my man. He said his wife is dead! So that's the story he's telling you? As she laughed. I left him. I had to get away. That sweet, loving and kind man I married turn into a monster. I feared for my life. So, I had to leave that was the worst choice I ever made. So why is that I replied? My son, I couldn't take him. He wouldn't let me. We also have a 5-year-old daughter. Wait another child? Yes, he told me to take her and get out his face, or he would beat both of us.

Ma'am I don't know what to tell you. I just can't believe my Quincy would ever do such a thing. Trust and believe me he's a monster.

Hey who's she? Angela said walking up towards the table. I ignored her and continued to talk to Brittany. Ok, look so what if you're telling the truth. What can I do about it? I need your help; I want my son back. Why you didn't call the police? Quincy have too many connections I tried everything, so you are my last option. So, if I was to help you, then you're telling me he's dangerous. I don't need those kinds of problems. Let me ask you a question, did he ask you to marry him?

Oh so y'all heifers talking about your new lil boo? Excuse me, yes bitch this is Quincy wife the one who was supposed to have died. Girl ain't that some shit, look Katie I'm going to give you my number. If you think you could help me out, please let me know. Sorry I didn't mean to upset you, she ran off. I was stunned I didn't have no words to say Katie's, Angela kept calling my name, but I just couldn't answer. Did this just really happen? I'm going to kill this son of a bitch! I have so much anger just boiling inside of me. I know there's two side to every story. Yes, Katie keep telling yourself that because I am on war page. I always find myself back to the beginning, stuck on stupid. How could I let another man come along and fill me up with lies? Damn I thought I found real love and happiness, but it's obviously I didn't.

A Sucker for Love That Is Me.

AUTHOR KESHIA MASON

www.ingramcontent.com/pod-product-compliance
Lightning Source LLC
Chambersburg PA
CBHW030534020726
47494CB00004B/1361